Fun China

CHINESE FESTIVALS

Written by **Alice Ma**
Illustrated by **Sheung Wong**
Reviewed by **Judith Malmsbury**

Sun Ya Publications (HK) Ltd.
www.sunya.com.hk

Today is New Year's Eve.
Charlie and Ying Ying are counting down until midnight.

"Five…four…three…two…one…midnight!"
Suddenly, a friendly creature appears.

The children's eyes widen with wonder.
They are very eager to find out more.

Let's start with the Chinese New Year.
It is a time when Chinese people
celebrate the start of the lunar calendar.
The Chinese New Year usually falls in January or February.
Families gather to share yummy food and exchange gifts.
Children get red packets filled with money from their parents.

But that's not all.
There are sparkling firecrackers and lion dances.
They can scare away bad luck and bring good fortune.

Next, we have the Lantern Festival.
It marks the end of the Chinese New Year celebrations.

On this day, people light and send up colourful lanterns into the sky for good luck.
Let's enjoy this happy festival with pretty lanterns and our family and friends.

We also enjoy solving lantern riddles.
Here's one:
sometimes round
and sometimes curved,
sometimes visible
and sometimes not.
What is it?

Answer: The moon

In early April, there is a Chinese festival called the Tomb Sweeping Day.
It is a day when families remember their loved ones who have passed away.

People visit their ancestors' graves
and sweep away dust and leaves.
They also bring flowers and food to show love and respect.
Although our ancestors are no longer with us,
they live on in our hearts forever.

Do you know about the festival that comes next?
It is the Dragon Boat Festival,
which usually takes place in June.

On this day, people race long dragon boats on the river.
They also eat sticky rice dumplings.
You can taste pork, beans and mushrooms
inside these yummy pyramids.
Come join the celebration and experience the Chinese tradition!

Kids, listen up. It is storytelling time!
Once upon a time,
there were a cowboy and a knitter who lived in the sky.
They loved each other, but were separated
by a big river called the Milky Way.
They could only meet once a year.

Over time, this sad story became the Chinese Valentine's Day.
It happens in August instead of February.
So, next time, show your loved ones, like your parents,
some extra love on this special day!

Are you ready for the Mid-Autumn Festival?
It takes place when the moon is super bright and round.
Usually, it is in September or October.

During the Mid-Autumn Festival,
we eat tasty treats called mooncakes.
Families get together to look at the full moon.
Let's enjoy this good time and have lots of fun!
Mooncakes are yummy.
I like them very much!

Every country has a special day to celebrate,
and China has its own too.
It is called the National Day that happens on 1st October.
But guess what?
The celebration lasts for a whole week!

People in China have a big parade with colourful decorations.
They enjoy shows and concerts as well.
It is like a giant birthday party for the country!

Ready for some fun?
We are going to climb a hill and fly kites!
This is a tradition for the Double Ninth Festival,
which usually happens in October.

“Double nine” means a long life in Chinese.
During this meaningful festival, we show respect
to older people and pray for their good health.
Next time, why don’t you take your grandparents out
and give them a big hug on this day?

Do you know about the Winter Solstice?
It is the day when the daytime is the shortest
and the nighttime is the longest.

People all around the world
celebrate the Winter Solstice differently.
The Winter Solstice always falls in late December.
In China, we like to spend time with family and have a big meal.
It is a happy time of the year when we feel warm
in our hearts, even though it is cold outside.

Let's celebrate the last festival of the year in China – the Laba Festival! At this festival, we say thank you for the harvest we had during the year. Meanwhile, we hope for more next year.

We eat a tasty porridge made with rice, beans and nuts
on this special day.
It means good luck, health and happiness.
Would you like to try some?

One festival follows another.
Charlie and Ying Ying learned about
many Chinese festivals from Dragon C.

As the night ends, they go to bed happily.
Both of them are dreaming of
the next festival they will celebrate.
Kids, which festival do you want to dream about?

English - Chinese Glossary of Chinese Festivals

Chinese New Year

TC 農曆新年

SC 农历新年

nóng lì xīn nián

Lantern Festival

TC 元宵節

SC 元宵节

yuán xiāo jié

Tomb Sweeping Day

TC 清明節

SC 清明节

qīng míng jié

Dragon Boat Festival

TC 端午節

SC 端午节

duān wǔ jié

Chinese Valentine's Day

TC 七夕

SC 七夕

qī xī

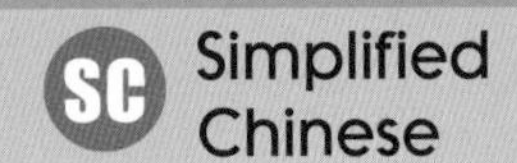

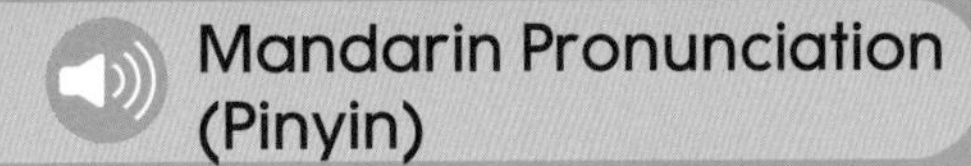

Mid-Autumn Festival

TC 中秋節

SC 中秋节

zhōng qiū jié

National Day

TC 國慶

SC 国庆

guó qìng

Double Ninth Festival

TC 重陽節

SC 重阳节

chóng yáng jié

Winter Solstice

TC 冬至

SC 冬至

dōng zhì

Laba Festival

TC 臘八節

SC 腊八节

là bā jié

Fun China
Chinese Festivals

Author
Alice Ma

Illustrator
Sheung Wong

Reviewer
Judith Malmsbury

Executive Editor
Tracy Wong

Graphic Designer
Aspen Kwok

Publisher
Sun Ya Publications (HK) Ltd.
18/F, North Point Industrial Building, 499 King's Road, Hong Kong
Tel: (852) 2138 7998   Fax: (852) 2597 4003
Website: https://www.sunya.com.hk
E-mail: marketing@sunya.com.hk

Distributor
SUP Publishing Logistics (HK) Ltd.
16/F, Tsuen Wan Industrial Centre, 220-248 Texaco Road,
Tsuen Wan, N.T., Hong Kong
Tel: (852) 2150 2100   Fax: (852) 2407 3062
E-mail: info@suplogistics.com.hk

Printer
C & C Offset Printing Co., Ltd.
36 Ting Lai Road, Tai Po, N.T., Hong Kong

Edition
First Published in October 2023

ISBN: 978-962-08-8271-5

18/F, North Point Industrial Building, 499 King's Road, Hong Kong
Published in Hong Kong SAR, China
Printed in China